14 Feb 1992

for Max,

with all our love,

Mom & Dad

E

BRU

This 1990 edition published by JellyBean Press,
distributed by Outlet Book Company, Inc.,
A Random House Company, 225 Park Avenue South,
New York, New York 10003

ISBN 0-517-05213-X

8 7 6 5 4 3 2 1
Printed in Italy

BABAR ™

and His Friends

In Celesteville

Twin Books

JellyBean Press
New York

This morning, because it is so beautiful,

 ,  ,  and

have decided to go for a long walk through the

pleasant streets of Celesteville.

Zephir prefers to follow everyone on his  ;

it's less tiring and more fun.

All their friends say good morning to them;

even Lord Rataxes waves from his  .

"Hurry up, Flora. Don't dawdle," says Babar.

But Flora doesn't hear him: she is busy making

friends with the spotted .

Babar, Pom, Flora, Alexander, bicycle, car, dog

"Hey! Look at me!" calls foolish Zephir. Oh, no!

He is standing up on his  !

Pom and Flora find this very funny, but not Babar.

"Look out!" cries Babar, as Zephir almost runs

right into a  . That was close!

And Zephir's has fallen into the street.

A  brakes suddenly, and the bus driver

is very angry with Zephir. So is Babar!

Alexander hasn't seen anything; he is chasing

a red through the flower bed. But it

has already flown away.

bicycle seat,
motorcycle, beret,
bus, bird

Zephir falls off his bike onto the sidewalk.

Luckily, a passing  is

stopped by an onlooker very near the scene.

"There you go," says the driver, who has put

a 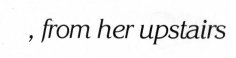 on Zephir's finger. "Soon it won't hurt

anymore, but stop playing acrobat."

The  , from her upstairs ,

calls "Poor Zephir!" and runs downstairs to him.

"Come in, please: is here to keep

you company." "I feel fine now," protests Zephir.

"But look at my poor twisted bicycle..."

ambulance,
bandage,
Old Lady,
window, Arthur

Zephir thinks he will rest a while with Arthur.

The others, joined by the Old Lady, continue their

walk. A  helps them to cross the street,

but little Flora doesn't watch where she's going.

"The  is red, but still, be careful," calls Babar.

"Flora, stay in the crosswalk."

Alexander likes the policeman's beautiful  .

"Some day I will be a policeman, too," he says.

"And I'll have a just like yours." He

stops for a moment to give himself courage,

then asks, "Sir, could I please blow your ?"

policeman, traffic light, uniform, cap, whistle

"Let's go to the park,"suggests Babar, and

everybody agrees, especially the children.

The Old Lady and Babar decide to sit down on

a park  near an elderly gentleman

who is trying to read a  despite the noise.

"Look how fast I'm going," cries Alexander loudly,

zooming down the .

"Look at me! Look at me!" cries Pom, pumping hard.

"See how high I can go!"

The  makes Flora feel dizzy, so

she prefers smelling the flowers on the .

bench, newspaper,
slide, swing,
bush

"This  : is it yours?" Pom asks a little hippo,

who is waving his arms in his  .

The mother hippo thanks Pom, but tells him that

"He is still too little to play with you. And besides,

it's lunchtime. He is about to have his  ."

"This little is hungry!" cries Flora,

feeding it some bread crumbs.

Babar, who is crossing the  ,

tells Flora and Alexander to pay attention to

the big bird—a  swimming toward them.

"She is greedy," says Babar. "She eats everything!"

rattle, stroller,
bottle, duckling,
bridge, swan

Not far from the park, Pom spots a cafe with an

empty  on the sidewalk. "Papa,"

he asks, "isn't it time to eat? I'm hungry!"

"So am I," says Babar. "Let's all sit here under

the striped  and have a cold drink."

The waiter soon comes out to take their order.

Flora says, "I would like a big of fresh,

cold orange juice to drink through a ."

Pom is so hungry that he orders not only some

juice, but a strawberry  as well.

"I would like a cup of tea," says the Old Lady.

table, umbrella,
glass, straw,
ice cream cone

All of a sudden. a  jumps onto the table,

chased by a big angry dog on a leash!

What noise! Everyone begins to shout at once.

"Look out for that !" calls Alexander

to the waiter, who is arriving with the tea.

Too late! He stumbles and breaks the chair.

In falling, he drops the , along with

everything on it. A real disaster!

The overturns in the street and the

is smashed into several pieces. Just then, they all

hear the loud noise of a siren...

cat, chair,
tray, teapot,
cup

"What's happening now?" asks Babar, as they

watch the arrival of the  .

"Look, Papa, the cat has climbed high up into

that big  ," says Flora. "It can't get

down, and it's mewing."

After raising the long 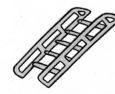 , a brave young

 climbs up to reach the cat. But look!

Now the cat doesn't want to come down!

It has spotted a  on a branch to play

with. The fireman grabs the cat by the back of its

neck. "Bravo!" Pom calls to him after the rescue.

fire engine, tree,
ladder, fireman,
nest

At last, everyone finishes his snack. No longer

hungry, they resume their walk. Window

shopping at the  shop for women,

the Old Lady tells Flora, "I don't know which one

I like best . . . Perhaps it's this pretty ?"

Flora likes high-heeled  with bows.

"Oh! If only I were grown up!" she sighs.

Celeste chooses a with a pretty veil.

Pom and Alexander are much more interested

in the window of the sweet shop next door.

"Look at that huge !" they exclaim.

BOUTIQUE

CANDY S

*dress, skirt,
shoes, hat,
lollipop*

"Look out for this big  of mine, Madame!"

The Old Lady turns around and sees someone

pasting a  in French on the garage.

To read it better, she finds her  .

"A supermarket here! What a good idea!" she says.

Here comes Rataxes, looking quite angry. He is

going to a  out in front of the garage.

"I have run out of gas," he fumes. "Please fill

up this 5-gallon  , and be quick about it."

Alexander can't help himself: He bursts out laughing.

But Rataxes glares at him. He's not amused.

brush, poster,
glasses,
gas pump, gas can

Following the road, Babar, the Old Lady and the

children suddenly see a very tall 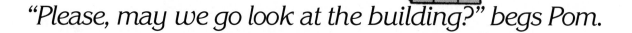 .

"Please, may we go look at the building?" begs Pom.

In front of a  that is dumping sand

stands a young elephant in a . He is

talking to Cesarine, the giraffe. Why, it's Arthur!

"Zephir was feeling better," he explains to Babar.

"We wanted to see this new house Cesarine is

building, and especially the  ."

"Hello! Here I am," calls Zephir, waving at them

with a big . "I'm helping the masons."

crane, truck,
hard hat,
bulldozer, brick

Somewhere nearby, they hear a strange noise.

"It must be a  ," says Babar. "Let's

go say hello to the carpenter."

"What are you making of the  ?"

Flora asks him, while she watches him work.

"I'm planning to put up a  like

that one hanging on the wall," he explains.

"Let him do his work, children," says Babar. "Pom,

put down the . We must hurry to

the museum. Soon it will be time to close."

"Wait! I will put in one and then come."

In front of the city museum, a big hippopotamus

carrying a  bumps into the Old Lady.

"Oh, forgive me. Are you all right?" he asks her.

"I'm sorry—I'm in a hurry to catch a train!"

"There is a  over there," Arthur says.

"Thank you," replies the hippo. Before he leaves,

he picks up her for the Old Lady.

The museum guard tries to send Babar and the

children away but Babar looks at his  .

"It isn't too late, I hope. Let me have six tickets

of admission, please." He takes out his  .

suitcase, taxi,
purse, watch,
wallet

In the museum, they are the last visitors of the

day. Alexander spends a long time gazing at the

big  of Babar as a young king.

Zephir is having fun sliding on the floor—until he

slips and bumps into a  . How clumsy!

Pom is happy that they have let him hold the

to the cloakroom. He will guard it very carefully.

"This new marble  of you is well done!" the

Old Lady tells Babar, who blushes at the compliment.

Flora has found a magnificent gold in a

glass case. She would like to have it.

painting, sword,
ticket, statue,
bracelet

Everybody is getting tired, but not too tired to go to

the toy store, because the Old Lady has kindly

offered to give each of the children a present. "A

blue ! Just what I wanted!" says Arthur.

Flora has already seen a with curly hair.

"Oh, dear!" thinks Babar, as he sees Pom coming

with a new . "My poor ears. . .!"

"May I have a walking  ?" Alexander

asks the Old Lady, who is waiting for them over

by a 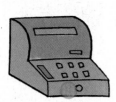 . "It's very funny." And Zephir

has discovered a dancing monkey

tennis racket,
doll, drum,
robot,
cash register,
puppet

"Let's go to the market now," says Babar. "But we

mustn't get home late. Celeste is waiting for us."

"How much does just one weigh?" asks Flora.

"Let me have it," says the grocer, and he puts it

on the  . "You see, it's not very heavy."

But what has happened to Zephir? Oh, no!

He has fallen down —and his  has

spilled. "Oh! My head," he groans. "I never noticed

that  . I walked right into it. And after

my bag broke, I stepped on my  ."

Poor Zephir. It just isn't his lucky day.

lemon,
scale, paper bag,
lamppost,
banana

Everyone has returned home to the palace.

"Happy Birthday, Mama!" cry Pom and Flora,

giving Celeste a fresh  .

"My birthday! I had forgotten all about it." She

unties the  on Alexander's present,

while Arthur comes in quietly, holding behind

his back a big  of colorful flowers.

"Oh, thank you, Arthur! I must put them into my

new  immediately. You are spoiling me."

The Old Lady is taking a dress from a 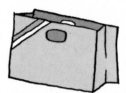 ,

when, from behind the door, there comes a noise. . .

pineapple, ribbon,
bouquet, vase,
package

A crowd of journalists soon invades the palace.

A reporter holds up a  before Celeste.

"Could you say a few words here by the 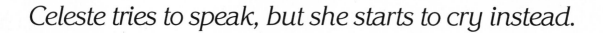 ?"

Celeste tries to speak, but she starts to cry instead.

She has to take out a  .

At the same moment, General Cornelius has

unrolled a big  from which to read his

speech. "We are proud to present our queen with

this beautiful portrait by the artist Justinien. . ."

"Don't move!" the photographer interrupts rudely.

"Look up into the  !"

microphone,
TV camera,
handkerchief,
scroll, camera

Night has fallen and peace is restored at last.

In the sky, a blue  flies over, singing.

From the balcony, Babar and his family watch

the setting over Celesteville.

"Look at that bulky old  of Cesarine's,"

says Pom. "The new one will be much better."

"Where is it?" asks Celeste. "I cannot see very far:

The  of the factory is smoking again."

"It's there, behind that ," says Babar.

"Do you know what I think is even more beautiful?"

asks Alexander very seriously. "The !"

bird, sun,
building, chimney,
weather vane,
TV antenna